Dear Parent:
Your child's love of reading starts here!

Every child learns to read in a different way and at his or her own speed. Some go back and forth between reading levels and read favorite books again and again. Others read through each level in order. You can help your young reader improve and become more confident by encouraging his or her own interests and abilities. From books your child reads with you to the first books he or she reads alone, there are I Can Read Books for every stage of reading:

SHARED READING
Basic language, word repetition, and whimsical illustrations, ideal for sharing with your emergent reader

BEGINNING READING
Short sentences, familiar words, and simple concepts for children eager to read on their own

READING WITH HELP
Engaging stories, longer sentences, and language play for developing readers

READING ALONE
Complex plots, challenging vocabulary, and high-interest topics for the independent reader

ADVANCED READING
Short paragraphs, chapters, and exciting themes for the perfect bridge to chapter books

I Can Read Books have introduced children to the joy of reading since 1957. Featuring award-winning authors and illustrators and a fabulous cast of beloved characters, I Can Read Books set the standard for beginning readers.

A lifetime of discovery begins with the magical words **"I Can Read!"**

Visit www.icanread.com for information on enriching your child's reading experience.

For Caleb, Isla, and Ariella.
Enjoy!
—R.S.

Splat the Cat: I Scream for Ice Cream

www.icanread.com

Library of Congress Control Number: 2014952531
ISBN 978-0-06-229419-7 (trade bdg.)—ISBN 978-0-06-229418-0 (pbk.)

15 16 17 18 19 SCP 10 9 8 7 6 5 4 3 2 1 ❖ First Edition

I Can Read!™ BEGINNING 1 READING

Splat the Cat

I Scream for Ice Cream

Based on the bestselling books by Rob Scotton

Cover art by Rick Farley

Text by Laura Driscoll

Interior illustrations by Robert Eberz

HARPER

An Imprint of HarperCollins*Publishers*

SCHOOL BUS

Splat the Cat beamed
in the back of the bus.
His class was on a field trip
to the ice cream factory!

"I could eat four ice cream cones
a day!" said Splat.
"I could eat fifteen!" said Plank.
"And I could eat all yours
and a million more!" said Spike.

Kitten licked her lips.

"I scream! You scream!

We all scream for ice cream!"

the friends cried.

At the ice cream factory,

ice cream swirled in big vats.

Pipes steamed.

Nozzles gleamed.

“Wow,” said Splat.

“What a dream!”

The factory manager greeted them.
"I am Mr. Jellybean," he said.
"Who wants a tour?"
"Hooray!" sang the cats.
"I scream! You scream!
We all scream for ice cream!"

Mr. Jellybean led the class
to a back room.
The cats' faces fell.
There was a chalkboard,
chairs, desks . . .
but no ice cream to be seen.

Mr. Jellybean cleared his throat.
"First, let's talk
freezers," he said.
"Some are big. Some are small.
All are extremely cold."

MR. JELLYBEAN

Mr. Jellybean talked on and on.

He seemed to love his freezer theme.

But the cats did not.

Their eyes glazed over.

Their heads drooped.

Splat began to daydream
that he was making ice cream.
He closed his eyes
and leaned against a big red button.

BEEEEP!

Alarms blared.

Lights beamed.

Splat jumped and screamed!

Steam puffed out of a big pipe.

Then—SPLAT!

Ice cream streamed out!

It became a huge ice cream wave . . .

that grew . . .

and grew . . .

and flooded the factory.

"Now *that's* a lot of ice cream," said Plank, taking a taste.

"Yum!"

"Wh-what happened?"

Mrs. Wimpydimple asked.

"I don't know,"

said Splat from under the chocolate chips.

The class cleaned themselves up.
Mrs. Wimpydimple counted heads.
Everyone was there, except . . .

"Seymour!" Splat screamed.

"I have to find Seymour," he said.

He ran back toward the door.

"Wait!" Kitten cried.

"We'll come with you!

We're a team, after all."

Inside, the team checked out
the ice-creamy mess.
“Let’s look,” they said.

“Be careful,” Splat said.
“Seymour is so small
we may not see him
under all this ice cream.”

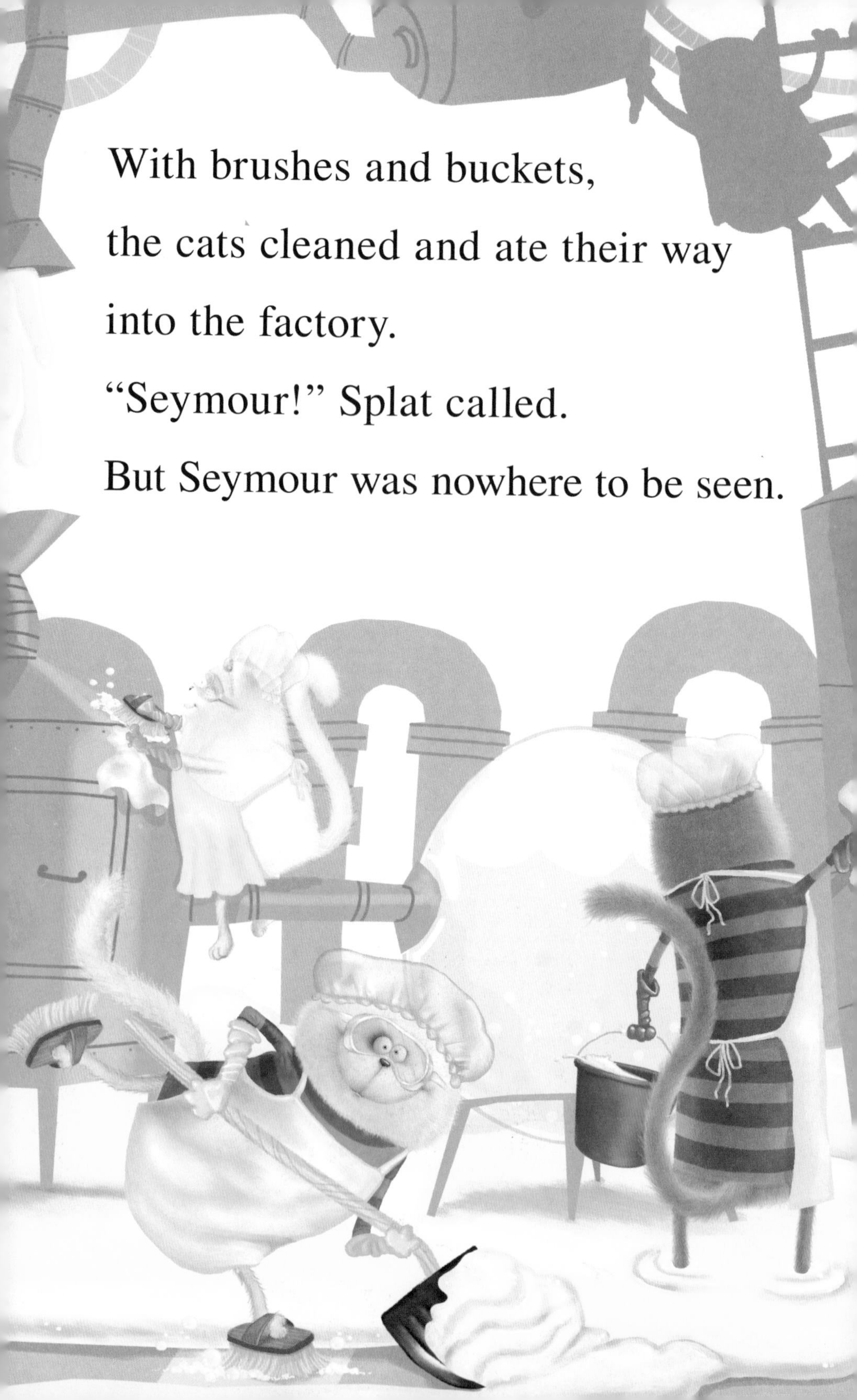

With brushes and buckets,
the cats cleaned and ate their way
into the factory.
"Seymour!" Splat called.
But Seymour was nowhere to be seen.

Then the team cleaned and ate
their way through the next room.
"Seymour!" Splat called again.

The team continued
until the factory gleamed.
But it seemed Seymour
wasn't anywhere
under all that ice cream.

Just then
a blob of whipped cream
fell onto Splat's head.
Splat looked up.

There was Seymour—

He was way up on a beam!

He couldn't call out.

His mouth was full of ice cream.

Seymour leaped into Splat's paws.

Then Mr. Jellybean thanked the team.

"The factory is so clean.

How can I repay you?

Would you like some ice cream?"

The cats all groaned.

“NO MORE ICE CREAM!” they said.

“For now . . . ,” whispered Seymour.